3

POKéMON

THE LOST RIOLU

Adapted from the two-part episode "Pokémon Ranger
and the Kidnapped Riolu!" by Helena Mayer

SCHOLASTIC INC.

NEW YORK   TORONTO   LONDON   AUCKLAND

SYDNEY   MEXICO CITY   NEW DELHI   HONG KONG

No part of this work may be reproduced in whole or in part, stored in a retrieval system, or transmitted in any form or by any means, electronic, mechanical, photocopying, recording, or otherwise, without written permission of the publisher. For information regarding permission, write to Scholastic Inc., Attention: Permissions Department, 557 Broadway, New York, NY 10012.

ISBN: 978-0-545-17723-8

Published by Scholastic Inc.
SCHOLASTIC and associated logos are trademarks and/or registered trademarks of Scholastic Inc.

12 11 10 9 8 7 6 5 4 3 2 1   10 11 12 13 14 15/0

Designed by Henry Ng.
Printed in the U.S.A.
This edition first printing, January 2010

Chapter 1

The moon was full. The stars were bright. Pokémon across the land were sleeping peacefully. But something wasn't right.

In a far, forgotten corner of the countryside, there was a dark fortress. Inside that fortress huddled a sad, lost Pokémon. It was a Riolu, a small, blue Fighting-type Pokémon.

And it was trapped.

Riolu didn't know where it was, or how it had gotten there. It just knew it was a prisoner. It had been for a very long time.

Suddenly, an alarm blared. A fireball tore through the prison wall. It left behind a giant hole. Riolu jumped to its feet. It climbed through the hole and started to run.

It was free!

But it wasn't safe, not yet. Alarms were

screaming. Guards and Pokémon raced back and forth. Floodlights swept the grounds, searching for Riolu.

Riolu tried not to be afraid. It just ran and ran as fast as it could. Out of the fortress, through the grounds. And finally beyond them, into the moonlit fields.

"There it is!" a guard shouted, spotting Riolu. "RX1!"

A man in a white coat stood behind him. "The RX1 is a *priceless* research tool!" he hissed. "Get Riolu back *at once*!"

The floodlights caught Riolu in their beam. The Pokémon froze in the light, trembling. It was terrified they would capture it again. But before they could, a Golem stepped out of the darkness. The Golem looked like a pile of rocks come to life. It shot a ball of fire at the fortress. The guards and the man in the white coat dove out of the way. That gave Riolu all the time it needed.

It raced across the field, tramping through high grass. The guards chased it.

Riolu was tired and lost. It didn't know how

much longer it could run. Suddenly, a truck skid-ded to a stop right in front of it.

Men in uniform piled out of the truck. They looked like soldiers. Each wore a patch on his chest. The patch was the familiar yellow, blue, and orange crest of Riolu's homeland. The Golem was by their side. Riolu realized these were the men who'd helped it escape. They must be on its side!

So it let them load it into the back of the truck. They slammed the door behind Riolu, locking it in.

The back of the truck was nearly empty. It was

a big space for such a small Pokémon. Riolu sat down. It was exhausted, and it had wounded its left arm in the escape. It closed its eyes. Finally, it could rest.

But before Riolu fell asleep, something happened. An eerie green light flashed across its face. A vision burst into its head. It was the men who were driving the truck. Riolu saw their faces clearly. It heard their voices.

"Excellent!" one of the men said. "Riolu *finally* belongs to me!" The man wasn't dressed in uniform like the others. Instead, he wore all black. His eyes were hidden by dark glasses. "And there'll be no doubt about who gives the orders," the man said, and began to laugh. The other men joined him.

"What a fool!" one of the soldiers said, chuckling. "Riolu trusted us *completely*!"

"Promising to *help* Riolu doesn't mean we'd send it home," added one of the other soldiers. "Poor thing." His voice dripped with sarcasm.

As the men laughed, they ripped the blue and yellow patches off their uniforms. Riolu realized that these men weren't from its homeland after all. And they *definitely* weren't trying to help Riolu escape.

So it would have to escape without their help.

Riolu squeezed its eyes shut and unleashed an Aura Sphere attack. A giant blue ball of energy blew open the back door of the truck. The truck skidded to a stop, nearly tipping over. Riolu jumped out. As soon as its feet hit the ground, it ran.

Two soldiers hopped out of the truck. They gaped at the destroyed doors.

"Riolu's escaped!" one of them said, shocked. "It must've overheard us talking!"

The other shook his head. "I can't believe it broke through this reinforced metal. Amazing!"

The man in black didn't have time for their disbelief. "Enough talk!" he snapped. "Get going. Riolu must not get away!"

"Sir!" the soldiers shouted in unison. They obeyed his order, rushing into the fields after the Pokémon.

Once he was all alone on the deserted road,

the man in black smiled. "So *this* is its power. It's even more than I dreamed!" He gazed across the dark field, impatient for his men to bring back Riolu. The Pokémon was too valuable to lose. "I *must* have Riolu for my own!"

Chapter 2

Ash, Brock, and Dawn hiked through a dense forest. They were journeying through the Sinnoh Region. Ash was determined to join the Sinnoh League. Pikachu, Ash's little yellow Electric-type Pokémon, perched on his shoulder. Dawn's Piplup tottered along next to the friends. Everyone was cheerful. It was a beautiful day.

Just then, Ash stumbled. A weird feeling swept over him. It felt like something was crawling inside his head.

"Ash, is something wrong?" Dawn asked.

"Uh, nope," Ash said quickly. He decided he must have imagined it.

Just then, a Pokémon popped its head out from behind a bush. A moment later, the Poké-mon stepped into their path.

"Whoa, what's that?" Ash said, his eyes wide. The strange Pokémon had long floppy ears and a dark stripe over its eyes.

"A Riolu!" Brock said in a hushed voice.

Dawn had never seen one before. "Riolu?"

Ash wanted to know more about the Pokémon, too. He pulled out his Pokédex.

"*Riolu, the Emanation Pokémon,*" the Pokédex explained. "*When sad or scared, Riolu's aura becomes stronger as a way of signaling its allies.*"

Ash suddenly understood where that weird

feeling had come from. "So *that* was it," he exclaimed. He was amazed that the Riolu had tried to communicate with him. He wondered if it would happen again. But instead, the Riolu clutched its left arm. It sank to its knees with a pitiful moan.

"Look, Riolu's hurt!" Brock said in alarm.

Ash rushed to help the Pokémon. He knelt before Riolu. "Let me help you! Are you okay?"

Riolu slapped him away.

"I'm trying to help," Ash insisted. He reached for Riolu's wounded arm.

A blue energy beam sizzled from Riolu's hand.

"Ash!" Brock shouted. But it was too late. The energy beam slammed into Ash. He flew backward and landed in a heap several feet away.

"Pika!" Pikachu yelped, running over to help its friend. Brock and Dawn came, too. They helped Ash off the ground.

"Don't worry, I'm okay," Ash said, in a shaky voice. His ears were ringing. He wobbled on unsteady legs. "*Man*, that was some move," he said in awe. This was one powerful Pokémon.

"That was an Aura Sphere for sure," Brock said. Now that he knew his friend was okay, he was excited about seeing such a cool attack in action.

"Aura Sphere, really?" Dawn asked, amazed.

"Yeah." Brock was sure. He was training to be a Pokémon breeder, and that meant knowing a *lot* about all kinds of Pokémon. "That move's normally learned after Riolu evolves into Lucario, but obviously not this time. Incredible!"

Dawn gasped. "Then that Riolu's really special."

"Special or not, Riolu needs a hand," Ash said, determined to try again. This time, he approached Riolu slowly, with his arms out to his sides. "C'mon, just relax," he said, in a soft, patient voice. "I know you're hurt, and I'm only trying to help."

Ash took a step toward Riolu. Then another. It looked like this time the Riolu might actually be ready to trust him.

But then Riolu attacked! A stream of blue fire streaked toward Ash.

Just as it was about to hit him, someone leapt in the way and knocked the beam off course. Ash stumbled backward, staring up at the helpful stranger. He was a little older than Ash and wore a long, green coat.

"Hey, everybody still in one piece?" the strange boy asked.

"Yeah," Ash said, confused. Where had the stranger come from? And what did he want?

Brock and Dawn wanted to know, too. Riolu took advantage of the distraction. It ran away into the forest.

"Riolu, wait!" Ash shouted. The Pokémon was hurt—it needed their help.

"Don't worry, I'll handle this," the strange boy assured them. He took off after Riolu.

"I wonder who that could be," Dawn said.

Ash didn't have time to worry about it. "C'mon, guys," he urged them. "We can't just stand here and do nothing when Riolu needs help!" He chased after Riolu and the stranger.

"But, Ash, wait!" Brock shouted.

Ash didn't wait. So Brock and Dawn had no choice but to follow.

Once they were gone, the bushes rustled. It wasn't the wind. It was Team Rocket. They had been watching the whole time.

"An Aura Sphere-toting Riolu is one rare and power-packed Pokémon, wouldn't you agree?" James asked. He smiled greedily.

Meowth, their talking Pokémon, bounced with excitement. "Yeah! And dat's da kind a power we need to pack!"

Jessie agreed. "We can't allow Riolu to languish with those lame losers." She thrust her fist in the air. "Team Rocket for the power play!"

Chapter 3

Ash looked everywhere for Riolu, but no luck. He was losing hope when a hand darted out from the bushes and yanked him to the ground. Ash yelped in surprise. The strange boy in the green coat was crouched behind a bush.

"You!" Ash said.

"I *told* you guys I'd take care of this, didn't I?" the boy said. He sounded annoyed that Ash had followed him.

Ash still didn't understand why they were hiding in a bush. "But—"

The stranger shushed him. He pointed toward the sky. Ash followed the boy's finger, and his jaw dropped in surprise. Riolu was perched on a tree branch high above their heads. His eyes were closed.

Soon Brock and Dawn caught up with them. Riolu hadn't moved.

"So is that *your* Riolu?" Dawn asked quietly.

The stranger shook his head. "Nope, not mine."

"So then it's a *wild* Riolu?" Brock sounded hopeful. He'd never seen a Pokémon like that in the wild before.

The stranger shook his head again. "Nope, not wild." His voice grew solemn. "All Riolu wants to do at this point is get back home."

Ash didn't get it. "Back home?"

But before the stranger could explain, a fleet of tanks rolled up to the tree. Riolu's eyes popped open as uniformed men piled out of the tanks.

Dawn tensed. "That's Pokémon Hunter J's goon squad!"

One of Hunter J's henchmen threw a Poké Ball. "Now, Crobat!" he shouted. The Poison-type Pokémon burst out of the ball. "Wing Attack, go!" The Crobat flapped its wings and flew straight into Riolu. It knocked Riolu out of the tree.

The little Pokémon fell a long way down, landing with a thud. It didn't move.

"Retrieve the target!" the head of the squad ordered.

"Those thugs are after Riolu!" Brock whispered from their hiding place.

"No way!" Ash jumped to his feet.

"Wait!" the stranger cried.

But Ash ignored him. He stormed into the clearing. "Stop it!" he shouted at Hunter J's squad.

The men looked annoyed, but not afraid. "Hey, kid, who're you?"

Ash knew they thought he wasn't a threat, because he was just a kid. But he was ready to prove them wrong. "Okay, Pikachu," he ordered. "Use Thunderbolt!"

Pikachu's powerful Thunderbolt sailed into the Crobat. The Bat Pokémon toppled out of the air and banged into a tank.

Before Hunter J's men could react, Riolu burst out of the bushes. Hovering in midair, it began firing Aura Spheres in all directions. Fireballs flew toward the hunters — and also toward Ash and his friends! Everyone cowered, trying to avoid the flames.

But when the attack ended, the goon squad was still standing.

"So that's the famous Aura Sphere," their leader said. "Impressive. Good power!" It made him even more determined to capture the Poké-mon. "Riolu's ours! Let's go!"

The hunter's men threw out more Poké Balls. The sky filled with Crobat after Crobat.

"Crooks!" Ash shouted angrily. "No way!"

He reached for a Poké Ball of his own. But the stranger stepped in front of him. "I won't allow it!" the stranger said sternly. He ripped off his green coat. Beneath it, he wore shorts and a red shirt. A strange mechanical glove wrapped around his right arm.

"It's a Vatonage Styler!" Brock exclaimed.

Dawn knew what that meant. "Then *he's* a . . ."

"Pokémon Ranger!" Ash concluded. None of them could believe it. Pokémon Rangers were Trainers who had dedicated themselves to protecting wild Pokémon. No one cared more about Pokémon than Rangers.

"Capture *on!*" the Ranger cried. He pointed his gloved hand at an Ariados that was hanging from a nearby tree. A beam of white light encircled the Pokémon. "Vatonage!" the Ranger shouted, as the Bug-and-Poison-type Pokémon absorbed

the light. "Capture complete. Ariados, use String Shot!"

The Ariados obeyed. It aimed its attack at the Crobat, binding them in thick loops of string. Unable to flap their wings, they dropped to the ground like stones.

Hunter J's men didn't know what to do. "What the . . . ?"

The Ranger wasn't done. He spotted a Nincada scuttling along the forest floor. "Capture on!" the Ranger shouted, aiming his glove. "Vatonage!" Quickly, the Nincada was captured. "Nincada, use Dig," the Ranger commanded.

The Nincada began digging furiously into the ground. It disappeared beneath the earth, tunneling toward Hunter J's men. A moment later, the ground beneath their feet exploded in a cloud of dust. The men dropped into an enormous sink-hole.

"Awesome!" Ash said.

Dawn clasped her hands in excitement. "Wow, seeing a Pokémon Ranger in action up close and personal like this is so *cool*."

"And he's no ordinary Pokémon Ranger, either," Brock pointed out. "He's a Top Ranger."

Ash hadn't heard of those. "A Top Ranger?" he asked.

"That's a Pokémon Ranger who's skilled enough to use a Vatonage Capture Styler," Brock explained.

Now that Hunter J's men were taken care of, the Ranger released the Pokémon he had captured. Then he knelt in front of Riolu. He took out a small, wooden Riolu-shaped doll and slipped it into a pouch. Then he looped the pouch around Riolu's neck. "You see, you can trust me, Riolu," he said gently.

The Riolu gazed up at the Ranger with large, red eyes. Finally, it let the Ranger lift it off the ground.

"There," the Ranger said in satisfaction. He glanced at Ash and his friends. "C'mon, follow me!"

They started running, heading deeper into the forest. They wanted to get the Riolu far away before Hunter J's men were back in action.

"So you came out here to help out that Riolu, right?" Ash asked, matching his pace to the Ranger's.

"Right!" the Ranger said. "The name's Kellyn. Hi there!"

"Hi," Ash said. "I'm Ash!" He was always happy to meet someone who liked Pokémon as much as he did.

Dawn waved at the Ranger. "And my name's Dawn."

"Nice to meet you, I'm Brock!" Brock said, trying to catch his breath. They were running as fast as they could

But no one was chasing them. Hunter J's soldiers were still trapped in the hole, screaming for help.

No one answered their pleas. But someone heard: Team Rocket. They were hiding, as usual. And they had seen everything.

"First we get preempted by a pack of Pokémon Hunter henchmen, and then we get upstaged by a Pokémon Ranger?" James said irritably.

Meowth pointed out the bright side. "When

dose heavyweights want what we want, we're barkin' up da right tree!"

Jessie clenched her fist. "Hunter J is going to *pay*. I'll turn the tables on her so fast, her head will spin."

"Bold!" James said, impressed. "But this is *Hunter J* you're putting away."

Jessie didn't care. "The *J* stands for *jerk*," she spat. "When I'm through flailing on her, she'll be *Pitiful* Pokémon Humble J!"

Chapter 4

They couldn't run forever. Riolu was wounded. So once they'd put plenty of distance between them and Hunter J's men, they stopped.

Ash and his friends waited along the bank of a wide river while Kellyn the Ranger tended to Riolu's wound. "Riolu, you'll be feeling better in no time," Kellyn promised, spraying medicine on the Pokémon's arm.

Riolu pulled away. He turned his back on the Ranger and gazed out at the water.

"It's gonna take time before Riolu can trust people again," Kellyn explained.

Riolu took out its little wooden doll. It clutched the doll to its chest.

"Hey, isn't that the doll you gave Riolu before?" Dawn asked.

"Yeah, it was a gift from the man who raised it," Kellyn said.

Ash wanted to know more. But before he could ask, that weird feeling swept over him again. Suddenly, he found himself in another time and place, in a strange house he'd never seen before. Riolu was there! There was an old man there, too, his eyes full of kindness. He handed Riolu a small wooden doll.

With a jolt, Ash was back in the present. He was pretty sure he'd just seen one of Riolu's *memories*.

He crept toward Riolu. "That's worth more to you than anything, right, Riolu?" he asked, pointing to the doll.

The little Pokémon turned to face him, its large red eyes blinking in surprise.

"You used your Aura to tell me that!" Ash said eagerly.

His friends were surprised. "Ash, what do you mean Riolu used its Aura?" Dawn asked.

"Riolu used its Aura to transmit its emotions and memories," Brock guessed. "Right, Ash?"

"Yeah!" Ash still couldn't believe he'd actually seen inside Riolu's head.

"That's incredible," Dawn gushed.

Kellyn nodded. "You see, an Aura's like a feeling or spirit. All living things have their own unique Aura." He rested a hand on Ash's shoulder. "Ash, my friend, it looks like your Aura and Riolu's Aura are a perfect match!"

"Yeah!" Ash exclaimed. He wasn't surprised there was a special connection between him and the Emanation Pokémon. He had sensed it from the start. He knelt beside Riolu. "I'll help get you home safe," he swore. "Don't worry about that Hunter J. You can trust me. *Promise.*"

The Ranger's Vatonage Capture Styler began to beep. He flipped it open to reveal a screen. "Kellyn here."

"Hi, it's Solana," a girl's voice said.

"Solana?" Ash said, hurrying to get a look at the screen. He grinned at the familiar face.

"If it isn't Ash and Pikachu!" Solana exclaimed. "It's been a long time."

Dawn swiveled her head back and forth between Ash and the screen. "Ash, you know a real-life Pokémon Ranger?" She craned her neck to get a glimpse of Solana. "Wow, a girl, and with such awesome clothes! My name's Dawn, nice to meet you."

Brock had already met Solana—and it was a meeting he had never forgotten. "Of course, I certainly hope you didn't forget little ole' me, Solana," he choked out, his throat closing up with nervousness. His heart was beating a million times a minute. His face flushed bright red.

"Of course not, Brock," Solana said cheerfully. "Still working to be a Pokémon breeder?"

"Yes, of course, though now I'm working on something else—" Brock took a deep breath. "And that's for you to use your Capture Styler to capture *me*!" He yelped and fell backward, as his Croagunk snuck up behind him, its jaws snapping. Brock couldn't believe it—why was he always embarrassing himself in front of the girls he loved?

Solana didn't even notice. "So, you're in the Sinnoh Region now. Working hard to join the Sinnoh League, I'll bet," she said to Ash.

He nodded. "Yup, that's the plan for sure."

"That's just great," Solana said. "Good luck! And Kellyn, with Ash being such an amazing Trainer, I'm sure he's going to be a big help to you."

Kellyn grinned at Ash. "Sounds good, Solana. Oh, yeah—what's the latest with the search?"

Solana grew serious. "We've determined the precise location of Pokémon Hunter J's client, and Officer Jenny and I are headed there now."

"Riolu's under our protection," Kellyn informed

her. "We're heading toward the rendezvous coordinates."

A rumble of thunder drowned out Solana's reply. Everyone looked up in surprise. The sky was clear. So where had the thunder come from?

A huge, dark shape blotted out the sun. It wasn't a storm cloud. And the rumbling wasn't thunder.

"It's Hunter J's ship!" Dawn cried.

"She finally arrives," Brock said, preparing to fight.

"Let's go," Ash said, in a determined voice. "For Riolu."

"Now, everybody needs to stay calm," Kellyn said quickly. "And do just what I say, okay?"

"Got it!" they all agreed. Whatever happened next, they would be ready.

High above the forest, Hunter J was ready, too. She sat on the bridge of her ship in a huge metal chair, like a throne. She had a purple uniform, purple hair, and a very angry expression on her face.

A large screen hung at the front of the bridge. Her lead henchman appeared on the screen, issuing his status report. "Sire, forgive me," he said nervously. "Our target managed to escape with a Pokémon Ranger. A *Top* Ranger to be exact."

Hunter J glowered. This was bad news. But it wasn't unexpected. "Was it Kellyn?" she asked.

"Yes, Sir," the man admitted. "And he was helped by a group of young punks!"

An image of Ash and his friends flashed across the screen. Hunter J had tangled with them before. "Not them *again*," she complained. "So you're saying *they're* your excuse for failure?"

"Negative!" the henchman said quickly. "We still intend to retrieve the target." The screen went black.

Hunter J was furious. "Top Ranger," she hissed, her fists clenched. She would *not* let him get away with her Riolu. Not without a fight.

Chapter 5

Kellyn loaded Riolu, Ash, Dawn, Brock, and their Pokémon into a boat and set sail down the river. Riolu sat very still in the front of the boat, watching the wooded countryside float by.

"This paradise kingdom is Riolu's home," Kellyn explained. "Riolu's official title is Inheritor of the Aura. It was carefully raised by its breeder."

Ash didn't understand. "Inheritor of the Aura?"

"Each royal generation uses Riolu's Aura to protect the kingdom," the Ranger said. "It's passed on and on, from generation to generation. And Riolu's next in line."

"*That's* why Riolu can use Aura Sphere!" Brock said. If Riolu was supposed to protect a whole kingdom, it made sense that it was more powerful than most Pokémon at its level.

"Riolu was kidnapped and locked up by people who planned to use its power for evil purposes," Kellyn said sadly. "But a *different* group of people orchestrated Riolu's breakout for their evil purposes, although it's obvious Riolu somehow managed to escape from them, too."

"And now this, hunted by a Pokémon Hunter!" Brock exclaimed. "No wonder it doesn't trust anyone outside its kingdom."

Dawn's eyes filled with tears. "What an awful way to live."

Ash felt sorry for Riolu. But more than that, he felt angry. "Selfish people mistreating Riolu like that—I can't *stand* it."

Kellyn agreed. "To transport Riolu safely back home, that's what my mission's all about. A recovery team from Headquarters is just up ahead—"

He stopped abruptly as the bottom of the boat suddenly bulged toward them. A moment later, a swarm of Sharpedo burst through the wood. The boat snapped in two. Everyone went flying into the water!

Only Kellyn managed to keep his grip on a piece of the boat. He and Riolu sped down the river, trying not to slam into the rocks. Sharpedo chased close behind.

Ash flailed in the water, trying to keep his head above the surface. He held tight to Pikachu even as the current tried to rip the Electric Poké-mon out of his hands. "What are they doing?" Ash shouted, kicking his legs to stay afloat.

A fleet of tanks pulled up along the bank of the river.

Brock recognized them. "Those Sharpedo belong to Hunter J!" he realized. "They've found us!"

Kellyn thought fast. He aimed his Capture Styler at a nearby Floatzel. It wriggled through the water and was soon under his control. "Now, Ash, to the other side, hurry!" Kellyn cried. "Floatzel, help out!"

Ash threw his arms around the Floatzel. It began to tow him across the river. But Hunter J's henchmen weren't about to let him anywhere near their tanks.

"Sharpedo!" the leader shouted. "Aqua Jet!"

The Sharpedo shot through the air on an enormous jet of water. They hit Ash like a tidal wave. He nearly went under.

"Pikachu, use Thunderbolt!" Ash cried, flailing in the churning water.

The Sharpedos launched another attack, but Pikachu was faster. It hit them with Thunderbolt, sending them flopping into the water.

"Floatzel, step on it!" Kellyn urged the Water-type Pokémon.

The Floatzel was fast, but not fast enough. A giant fireball crashed into the river. It sent a wall of water speeding toward Ash and his friends. The wave smashed down on their heads, nearly drowning them. When they resurfaced, Hunter J was waiting.

She hovered over them on the back of her Salamence. It was a giant blue lizard with massive red wings sprouting from its back. And its fiery Hyper Beam attack could be very harmful.

"I'm taking Riolu," Hunter J informed them.

"I don't think so," Dawn shot back. "Piplup, use BubbleBeam!"

The Water-type Pokémon shot a beam of bubbles at Hunter J.

"All right, Salamence, Hyper Beam!" Hunter J countered. The Salamence reared back and spit out a giant fireball. It collided with the stream of bubbles, unleashing an enormous plume of black smoke.

"Floatzel, Water Gun!" Kellyn commanded. The Floatzel poked its head out of the water and slammed the Salamence with a geyser of water. The Salamence jerked and shuddered. Hunter J nearly toppled off its back. But she caught her balance and retaliated, firing down at Ash and Kellyn with a beam that could turn them to stone.

"Quick, dodge it!" Kellyn shouted, helping Riolu avoid the beam. They made it to safety. But in the chaos, Riolu dropped its doll in the river.

Riolu watched in horror as the doll disappeared under the water. It couldn't stand losing its one connection to the past. So it jumped into the river and swam after the doll.

"Riolu!" Ash cried, as Hunter J sent her tanks in pursuit of the Pokémon. "Buizel, let's go," Ash ordered the Water Pokémon. They paddled down the river, trying to catch up with Riolu.

But Hunter J was determined to get there first. "Salamence, use Hyper Beam!" she commanded, aiming her Pokémon at the cliffs lining the river. A fireball crashed into the cliff wall. It exploded into a hail of rocks. They tumbled into the river, raining down on Ash and his friends.

"Piplup!" Dawn screamed as her Pokémon was nearly hit by a falling boulder.

By the time the rocks stopped falling, Hunter J was gone.

So was Riolu.

Chapter 6

Riolu paddled toward its lost doll, but the current kept carrying it further and further away. The doll plunged over a waterfall, and Riolu followed it down.

"Go!" Ash shouted at Buizel. They toppled over the edge of the waterfall. Ash bumped and bounced his way down the falls. He slammed into the rapids at the bottom. Water sloshed over his head. He gasped for air, trying to stay afloat. Then he spotted Riolu down river. The Pokémon disappeared beneath the water.

"Riolu's in trouble!" Ash cried. "Dive underwater!"

Ash drew in a deep breath. Then Buizel towed him underwater. Everything became very dark and very silent. Riolu drifted face down, its eyes closed. Ash struggled toward it, desperate to save his friend.

Just as Ash reached Riolu, another Aura flash hit him. Suddenly, he wasn't in the water anymore. He was in a pretty, peaceful village. Riolu stood in the garden of a cozy cottage, practicing its Aura Sphere attacks. Nearby, an old man sat beneath a tree, carving a wooden doll. Ash recognized him from the last memory he'd seen. His eyes were just as kind as before.

"It's finished, Riolu!" the old man said. A wide smile spread across his face. "Here, for you."

He handed the doll to Riolu. The Pokémon gaped at him, like it had never received a present before. It had never been so happy.

Then an armored truck pulled up to the house. A scientist in a white coat stepped out. He was surrounded by guards and an angry-looking Drowzee. It was a bulky yellow Pokémon with a long snout.

The old man stood up to face them. He looked suspicious. "Yes?" he asked.

Riolu was afraid of the strange men. He hid behind the old man's leg.

"Who are you people?" the old man asked.

"Give us Riolu," the scientist said sternly. "Or should I say, *Project RXI*."

The old man's face went pale. "You fools! Don't you realize that this Riolu is vital to the future of our kingdom?"

"Of course!" The scientist smiled evilly. "That's why we're here." He jerked his head at one of the guards in a silent command.

"Drowzee, Psychic!" the guard snapped.

As the Hypnosis Pokémon readied its Psychic attack, the old man pushed Riolu out of the way. "Quick, run away!" he shouted. Riolu didn't want to leave the man behind, but he had no choice. It began to run. The Drowzee attacked. The doll went flying out of Riolu's hand, and there was a blinding white light—

The memory ended. Riolu opened its eyes. It was lying on the bank of the river. Ash hovered over him anxiously.

"I'm glad you're awake, Riolu," Ash said. He had pulled the Pokémon out of the water just in time. "We were worried."

Riolu sat up. It looked around, panicked. Ash knew exactly what it was looking for. He showed Riolu the wooden doll that he had rescued from the river. "I'll tell you, Riolu," he said, "your home's a beautiful place. I can really feel it. I mean, its Aura." He pressed the doll into Riolu's palm. "This belongs to you. Now take good care of it."

Ash heard familiar voices coming from a nearby clearing. He crept closer and peeked through the bushes. It was Hunter J and her henchmen!

"We received a report they didn't turn up downstream," the leader reported. "They must have washed up somewhere in this vicinity."

Ash and the Pokémon stayed very, very quiet.

"Are you certain?" Hunter J asked.

The leader nodded. "There's no doubt about it."

Ash turned to Riolu and Pikachu. He gave them a silent signal. On the count of three, they started to run.

"It's them!" one of the henchmen shouted, catching sight of Ash racing through the forest. They were about to chase him. But Hunter J stopped them. She had a better idea.

A dangerous idea.

Chapter 7

Team Rocket stood in the forest, staring down into a giant hole. Their hands ached from gripping their shovels. Their backs were sore from digging. But the pit was finally done.

"I know this is what we *do*," James said nervously, "but will a pit trap bring down Hunter J?"

Jessie had no doubts. "Like rain from the sky!" she said confidently. "And once she's been pitted, the pouncing proceeds."

"Da twerps're toast, da Ranga gets routed, an' we get Riolu," Meowth cackled.

They waited eagerly for Hunter J to appear. But something else appeared first: fire! The forest blazed into flames.

"Well, it wasn't me!" James said quickly. None

of them knew where the fire had come from. But they knew it was getting closer.

"It's a wildfire!" Meowth cried. "No dancin', let's *move*!"

But the flames surrounded them. There was no escape. "Wherever we move, we'll be toast!" James yelped.

Jessie had an idea. "It's time to use our pit-digging expertise for self-preservation," she said. "Alley oop!"

She jumped into the pit.

James and Meowth looked at each other. They realized they had no choice. "Alley oop!" they shouted, jumping in.

"We're out of the soup!" James cried, safely hidden from the fire. "Yay!"

The Pokémon of the forest weren't so lucky. The flames crackled around them. The heat seared their skin. Their home was burning, and there was nothing they could do but run for their lives.

Ash, Pikachu, Buizel, and Riolu were trapped in the fire, too. But they knew this was no natural forest fire. This was Hunter J's work. She hovered over them, riding her fire-breathing Salamence.

"I warned you to stay out of my way," she reminded Ash.

Ash wasn't going to let her get away with this. He was going to fight back. He just wasn't sure how. "I'm taking care of Riolu!" he cried. "And you just ran outta luck!"

"Right." Hunter J laughed. "Salamence, use Flamethrower *now*!"

"Look out!" Ash cried, as a giant plume of flame raged toward them. They dove out of the way as the fireball tore through the trees.

"Buizel, Water Gun!" Ash ordered.

The Pokémon's blast of water was too weak to put the fire out. But it cleared a safe path for them to escape.

"Pikachu, Riolu, Buizel, let's go!" Ash urged them.

"Enough!" Hunter J shouted. She zapped Riolu with her immobilizing beam. Riolu's doll clattered to the ground as Riolu turned to stone!

"Riolu!" Ash cried. He scooped up the doll and raced toward Riolu. But Hunter J was ready for him. She had Salamence attack with Hyper Beam. Ash ducked to avoid it. Before he could fight back, Salamence unleashed another Flamethrower. Ash cowered away from the fire.

"I spared Riolu the pain and suffering from

the flames," Hunter J crowed. "You should be grateful."

"Who do you think you are?" Ash was outraged. He had to stop her. But the flames stopped him from getting any closer. "You're not getting away with this!"

But that's exactly what she did. "Mission complete," she reported to her goon squad. "Retrieve the target."

Ash couldn't do anything but watch as they carried Riolu away.

On the other side of the forest, Dawn, Brock, and Kellyn were worried about their missing friends. But they had a burning forest to deal with.

"Everyone over here!" Dawn called to the fleeing Pokémon. She waved them toward the river, where they would be safe from the fire.

"This way," Brock added. "Everyone keep calm."

Kellyn aimed his Vatonage Capture Styler at a cluster of three Blastoise. "All right, Blastoise, I need all of you to help. Capture *on!*" The white light encircled the Blastoise. "*Vatonage!* Capture Complete! Blastoise, use Rain Dance," he ordered them.

"Yes!" Brock thought it was a brilliant idea. "Blastoise's Rain Dance will put out the forest fire!"

The Blastoise had large shells with cannons poking out of them. The cannons shot puffs of cloud into the sky. The clouds swirled together and grew into a major storm. The sky darkened. Rain pelted the forest.

Dawn tried to reassure the worried Pokémon. "You're all going to be just fine," she promised.

As the flames died away, everyone celebrated. But Kellyn knew this was no natural wildfire. "I'm sure of it," he murmured. "This fire must've been the work of Hunter J. I'm worried about Riolu and Ash," he told Brock and Dawn. "Let's go!"

But they were too late. Hunter J was gone, along with Riolu. Ash and Pikachu had fled from the flames. Only Team Rocket was left behind, hiding in their pit. But Kellyn, Dawn, and Brock ran right past without noticing them. Thanks to the rain, the pit had filled with water. It looked like a tiny lake.

Team Rocket climbed out. They were soaking wet.

"All right, all right, who did the rain dance?" Jessie complained. Her hair stuck to her forehead. Water dripped down her face.

"Not me," James insisted. "I was a bit preoccupied . . . treading water!"

Meowth grinned. Being wet was better than being on fire. "Only one 'ting it coulda been. Da great Team Rocket water boy in da sky!"

Chapter 8

Ash used Chimchar to dig a tunnel through the forest. He and Pikachu followed Chimchar underground. They tunneled away from the flames. When they came aboveground again, the fire was out. "Hey, thanks to you using Dig, we're all safe and sound," Ash told Chimchar. "Now, take a nice rest."

Chimchar returned to its Poké Ball.

"Rain, huh?" Ash said, looking around at the damp, smoldering trees. "Good thing, since it's putting out the fire." They had tunneled all the way to the edge of the forest. Now they were at the top of a steep hill, looking down over a wide, grassy valley. "What's that?" Ash asked, staring down at an intimidating gray metal building in the center of the valley. He decided to find out.

"C'mon!" Ash urged Pikachu. They bumped and slid down the hill.

As he got closer to the building, Ash realized it wasn't a building at all. It was a *ship* — Hunter J's ship. Ash and Pikachu crept quietly toward the ship. They reached it just as an armored tank rolled up. A hatchway lowered, and the tank rolled into the belly of the ship. Ash and Pikachu slipped in just behind it. The metal door clanked shut behind them.

Meanwhile, Kellyn, Brock, and Dawn raced through the forest, searching high and low. A dark shadow passed over them. They froze and looked up. "That's Hunter J's ship!" Dawn cried.

Brock frowned. "Does that mean they got Riolu?"

As Hunter J's ship soared overhead, the hunter herself was giving a status report to her client: mission accomplished.

Riolu was still frozen. It had been placed in a

glass case that sat next to Hunter J on the bridge. A man in a black suit and black sunglasses peered down at them from the large screen. It was the same man who had helped Riolu break out of the research fortress. Soon he would have Riolu back again — for good.

"Most impressive the way you carried out your assignment as promised," he told Hunter J. "Obviously it was a wise decision to hire you."

Hunter J gave him an icy smile. She didn't know his name. She knew him only as the client. "Well then, there's the matter of payment."

But the client was suspicious of everyone, even Hunter J. He didn't want to get cheated out of his prize. "First I'd like to see Riolu move with my own two eyes, please."

"Of course." Hunter J unfroze Riolu's head. Below the neck he was still completely immobilized. But his eyes opened. His head swiveled to the left and to the right, searching desperately for some chance of escape. There was nothing.

The client finally smiled. "It's the real thing, all

right. Very well then, I'll arrange to get you your payment right away."

"I'll meet you at the rendezvous point," Hunter J said. Then she flipped off the screen.

As soon as the man's face disappeared, Ash and Pikachu burst out of their hiding spot. They had seen the whole thing — and now they were more determined than ever to save Riolu. Somehow.

"Riolu!" Ash cried, catching sight of the glass case that imprisoned his friend. "Let Riolu *go*!"

But Hunter J did the opposite. She froze Riolu again. He went completely still. Then Hunter J threw a Poké Ball at Ash. A Drapion burst out of the Poké Ball. It was a huge, purple Pokémon with sharp teeth and claws. "Drapion, grab him, now!" Hunter J commanded.

The Drapion snatched Ash with one of its giant pincers. It lifted him off the ground and began to squeeze. The pincers dug sharply into his chest. Ash squirmed and wriggled, but the Drapion held on tight.

"I've been aware of your little intrusion the whole time," Hunter J taunted him.

The Drapion squeezed even tighter. It was getting hard for Ash to breathe. "Why didn't you do something before?" he choked out.

Hunter J laughed. "So I could *personally* punish a young fool like you!"

Pikachu couldn't take it anymore. It leaped at Drapion and landed on the Poison-and-Dark-type Pokémon's head. It grabbed at Drapion's horns. Then Pikachu stabbed a fist into the Drapion's eye.

Drapion shrieked in rage and pain. It reared back and dropped Ash to the ground. Thanks to Pikachu, Ash was free!

Hunter J watched the whole thing with a calm smile. Like she had a plan.

Ash stood up, ready to fight. But a trapdoor opened beneath his feet. Ash and Pikachu dropped right through it. They plunged through a deep, dark pit. It seemed bottomless. And then the world filled with light—it was the sun. They had fallen right through the bottom of the ship!

"Pikachu!" Ash cried. He grabbed his friend as they plummeted to the ground. But he couldn't save Pikachu any more than he could save himself. They were falling too far, too fast. The ground sped toward them. "This could be it," Ash gasped. The wind stole the words out of his mouth.

Ash tried to prepare himself to crash. Suddenly, talons hooked into the back of his shirt, and lifted him up. He and Pikachu were flying!

Ash looked up to discover a Staraptor above him. It was a Normal-and-Flying-type Pokémon that was carrying him to safety. Kellyn was riding the Staraptor. He waved down at Ash and Pikachu. "Got you, Ash!" he called to his friend. "So are you two all right?"

"Yeah, thanks to you and Staraptor!" Ash couldn't believe the Ranger had showed up just in time. He was happy that Kellyn had saved his life. But he couldn't help thinking of Riolu.

Ash and Kellyn watched Hunter J's ship disappear into the distance. "They got away," Kellyn said sadly.

"Riolu's with J!" Ash told him. "And it's all because I messed up, big time."

"Ash, you shouldn't blame yourself like that," Kellyn said quickly. "Don't worry, we'll save Riolu, for sure."

Ash wished he could be so certain. He couldn't stop blaming himself. He'd had the chance to save Riolu, and he'd blown it.

Soon the Staraptor brought them back to the rest of their friends. Dawn was thrilled to see them. "Pikachu, Ash! I'm so glad you're all okay." She hugged them in relief.

"Thanks," Ash said. He still felt terrible.

Brock saw the look on his face. He understood. "I guess J must've escaped with Riolu."

Ash couldn't say it out loud. He just nodded sadly.

Now that they were all back on the ground, Kellyn could release the Predator Pokémon. "You were a big help, Staraptor. Thanks!"

As Staraptor flew away, Kellyn got a transmission from Ranger Solana. He flipped open the screen on his Vatonage Capture Styler.

"I'm so sorry, Kellyn," Solana said. "But unfortunately, J's client managed to escape!"

"What'd you say?" Kellyn blurted. He couldn't believe it.

"You see, Jenny and I did our best and got as close as we could, but . . ." Her voice trailed off.

"I see. The truth is, J stole Riolu from us as well," Kellyn admitted.

Solana was alarmed. The situation was even worse than she'd thought. "That's awful!"

"She's on her way to rendezvous with her client and then transfer Riolu," Kellyn said. "Then they'll probably cover their tracks, which of course means one thing . . ."

Dawn gasped. "That we'll have lost Riolu!"

Brock wrung his hands together. "Which means Riolu will never be able to get back to its kingdom!"

Ash was upset, too. But mostly, he was angry. "Yeah? There's no *way* I'm gonna let that happen!"

He *would* rescue Riolu — but first he had to figure out where Hunter J had taken it. And there was only one way to find out. He tipped his face up to the sky. Maybe this wouldn't work, but he was desperate. "Riolu, c'mon, let me know!" he cried, hoping that somewhere, somehow, the Pokémon would hear him. "Tell me where you are! Rioluuuuuu!"

He closed his eyes, waiting for the familiar feeling of Riolu's Aura. But nothing happened.

Ash sank to his knees in despair. He had failed. It was over. "Riolu, I'm sorry."

Dawn took a step toward him. She didn't know how to help her friend. "Oh, Ash . . ."

Ash wasn't ready to give up. "Riolu, if you can hear me somehow, tell me," he begged. "C'mon, *tell me!*"

At that moment, a psychic flash zapped over him. Suddenly, he wasn't in the forest anymore. He was in a vast desert, surrounded by sandstone cliffs — and Riolu was there, too.

"What is it?" Brock asked. "Hey, Ash!"

"Riolu!" Ash cried. "That's where you are!"

In his mind's eye, he could see every detail of the desert. He knew exactly where to find the little Pokémon.

"What, Ash?" Dawn asked.

Only Kellyn knew exactly what was happening. "You sense its Aura," he guessed, "don't you?"

Ash opened his eyes and leapt to his feet. "You're right—this way!" he told his friends. "Riolu's this way!" There was no time to waste. He charged into the forest.

As his friends hurried after him, Kellyn relayed their status to Solana. "We're on our way to free Riolu *right now*. Please inform headquarters for me!"

"Understood," Solana told him. "Good luck, Kellyn!"

Kellyn was pretty sure they would need it.

Team Rocket was hoping for some good luck of their own. They were hidden behind a bush, and they had been eavesdropping again.

"You realize if we follow in the twerps' wake we'll come across Hunter J and Riolu in one fell swoop," Jessie said, once they were alone.

"Gettin' our paws on dat power Pokémon'll kick us way up a notch!" Meowth agreed.

Only James wasn't sure they could handle it. "But what do we do now that our poor pit traps are waterlogged?"

"We don't stand around and whine," Jessie snapped. "Climb every mountain! Ford every stream! Rout Riolu!"

Chapter 9

Ash, Dawn, Brock, and Kellyn had wrangled a herd of Dodrio. They rode the three-headed Pokémon through the forest and into the desert. "Hang on, Riolu," Ash murmured, as they galloped past the towering sandstone cliffs he'd seen in his vision. "We're coming!"

"I still can't believe Riolu's Aura could reach Ash even though Hunter J's holding it prisoner," Dawn said.

"That just goes to show you how strong the connection is between Ash and Riolu," Brock pointed out. He was impressed. He knew that forming a connection with a Riolu was very rare.

"Riolu responded to Ash's thoughts," Kellyn explained. "Those thoughts, along with Ash's emotions, allowed Riolu to use its powerful Aura to transmit its whereabouts."

Ash was barely listening to his friends. All he could think about was the kidnapped Pokémon. "Riolu, don't worry," he said, wishing Riolu could hear him.

But maybe Riolu *could*. Ash got another flash from Riolu's Aura. The Pokémon was scared and lonely—but it knew Ash was on the way. "The Aura's stronger than before, so we're getting really close!" Ash told his friends. He urged the Dodrio to go faster. They just *had* to reach Riolu before it was too late.

Less than a mile away, Hunter J's ship materialized in a dusty canyon. She and her minions climbed out into the desert. "The client will be here any minute now," one of the goons informed her. As he spoke, an armored truck pulled up to the rendezvous spot. The man in black stepped out of the truck, joined by minions of his own.

"I'm terribly sorry to keep you waiting, Hunter J," he said, sounding not very sorry at all.

Hunter J issued a silent command to her troops.

"Right!" the leader snapped. He set Riolu's glass case down on the desert floor, halfway between Hunter J and the client. The client stepped forward eagerly and scooped up the case.

"We found ya, J!" Ash's voice echoed through the canyon.

Hunter J and the client looked up in surprise.

Ash and his friends perched on a cliff overlooking the kidnappers. "We won't let you get away with this!" Kellyn shouted.

The client clutched the glass case to his chest. "A Pokémon *Ranger?*" he asked Hunter J, enraged that his plans were going awry.

Hunter J brushed aside his concern. "Bah! Annoying brat."

Kellyn gave them one last chance to surrender. "Riolu needs to return to its kingdom, so give it back immediately — or else."

The client wasn't afraid. "No!" he cried defiantly. "I'll give you nothing!"

Ash was prepared. He threw out a Poké Ball. Staravia burst into the air. "Staravia, use Quick Attack!" Ash ordered. "Go!"

Staravia spread its wings wide and soared into the canyon. It flew straight into the client and knocked him into the dirt. The glass case rolled away.

Hunter J's men panicked. "What now?"

"We have our money, let's go," Hunter J decided. She scurried onto the ship, eager to get away from the fight.

The client's soldiers barely noticed. They were too busy helping their boss to his feet. As they did, Ash and his friends rode the Dodrio straight down the cliff. Soon they were face to face with the client.

"Riolu belongs to me and nobody else," the client informed them defiantly.

Ash caught sight of the glass case, tipped over on the ground. Riolu was still frozen inside. "Riolu!"

One of the soldiers tossed out a Poké Ball. "Golem, use Hyper Beam!" The giant Rock-type Pokémon exploded from the Poké Ball. His bright yellow Hyper Beam slammed into Ash and knocked him to the ground.

"Ash, Pikachu, hang on!" Dawn cried.

"Ash, are you all right?" Kellyn asked in alarm.

"Yeah." Ash stumbled to his feet.

The client had already snagged the case again. "I've finally gotten my hands on a Riolu who uses Aura Sphere!" he crowed. He turned to his soldiers. "I've got Riolu, let's go!"

But Ash had other plans. "You're not getting away!" he insisted. "All right, Staravia, slash their tires with Quick Attack."

The Staravia quickly obeyed, pecking jagged holes into the truck's tires. It lurched over to one side.

"What?" the client yelped. "Nooo!" Hunter J's ship was gone. The truck was out of commission. Which meant the client was stuck!

Or was he?

"Give Riolu back!" Ash commanded.

The client shook his head. "Forget about it. Get him!" he ordered his soldiers.

The soldiers lined up. Each of them tossed out a Poké Ball.

"Rhyhorn, let's go!"

"Graveler!"

"Nidoking!"

"Tyranitar!"

The client raised an arm in the air. A Fearow swooped down and grabbed hold. Before Ash could do anything, Fearow lifted the client and Riolu off the ground and flew them away.

"Riolu!" Ash screamed.

But it was too late. Riolu was gone. And the soldiers' Pokémon were ready to attack. Ash didn't know what to do. Should he stay here to help his friends fight? Or should he go after Riolu?

Before he could decide, a two-seated

motorcycle roared into the canyon. "It's Solana!" Kellyn shouted. And she wasn't alone. Officer Jenny was by her side.

"Kellyn, leave J to us," Solana said, leaping out of the motorcycle.

"You go after Fearow," Jenny added.

"C'mon, Ash, let's go!" Brock urged him.

"We'd better hurry," Kellyn said.

Ash agreed. "Right!" He and Kellyn leapt onto the Dodrio and rode off after Fearow and the client.

"No you don't!" one of the soldiers shouted after them. "Golem, Sandstorm. Quick!"

"You, too, Rhyhorn!" another soldier ordered.

But Dawn wasn't about to let them stop Ash and Kellyn. She stepped into their path. "Piplup, BubbleBeam. Now!" The stream of bubbles slammed into Rhyhorn and stopped his attack.

Brock and Jenny quickly joined the fight. "Growlithe, come on *out!*" Jenny said, throwing a Poké Ball.

Brock tossed one, too. "You, too, Croagunk. Let's *go.*"

Dawn had a feeling this was going to be a rough battle. "This isn't going to be easy," she said to herself. "I need *everyone*'s help." She released Buneary, Ambipom, and Pachirisu from their Poké Balls.

The canyon exploded with the sounds of battling Pokémon. Rhyhorn deployed a Fury Attack. Buneary countered with a Quick Attack. Tyranitar unleashed Thunder Fang and Sandstorm. But Croagunk took it down with a Mud Bomb. Ambipom hammered them with Fury Swipes and Growlithe tried its nearly unstoppable Flame Wheel attack. But nothing was enough to defeat the soldiers and their Pokémon.

"They're way too strong!" Dawn cried, ducking all the fireballs and energy beams.

Brock was running out of options. "How do we stand up to them?"

Solana had an idea. "Capture *on*!" she said, aiming at a wild Trapinch. Soon it was under her control. "Capture complete. Quick, Trapinch, use Rock Tomb!"

Trapinch shuddered with the effort. A huge

tombstone-shaped rock blasted out of the ground. It was followed by another, then another. Soon a wall of giant rocks encircled all the soldiers and their Pokémon. They were trapped inside!

The fight was over and won—but the client was still out there somewhere, and he still had Riolu. Brock and Dawn exchanged a worried glance. They knew Ash would do everything he could to rescue Riolu.

But what if it wasn't enough?

Chapter 10

"Stop *now!*" Ash shouted. He and Kellyn had almost caught up with the Fearow.

"Those stubborn pests," the client grumbled. He urged the Fearow to fly faster.

Kellyn decided to try a risky move. He rode his Dodrio right up the side of the cliff. When he was high enough, he took a flying leap. He and the Dodrio soared through the air—and landed on top of the Fearow!

The client didn't see it coming. "Wh-what the—?"

"Dodrio, Fury Attack!" Kellyn commanded. All three of the Dodrio's heads began pecking at the Fearow. It screeched and squawked, but Dodrio wouldn't give up. Soon the Fearow sank to the ground. It dumped the client off its back.

Ash caught up to him and hopped off his Dodrio. "Now give Riolu back!"

The client clasped the glass case even tighter. "Not in a million years," he swore. He ran away from Ash as fast as he could, and disappeared into a crack in the side of the cliff.

"Stop!" Ash shouted. "C'mon, Pikachu." They followed the client into the side of the cliff, and found themselves in a huge, dark cavern. There were a hundred places the client could have been hiding.

But the client wasn't hiding, he was running. Deeper and deeper into the cavern, until he found himself in a wide, open chamber with ten branching tunnels. "Now what do I do?" he wondered.

First, he had to stop Ash and Kellyn from coming after him. He turned toward the entrance to the chamber. Then he threw a Poké Ball and released Aggron. "Rock Smash, let's go!" he commanded. Aggron aimed his Rock Smash at the entrance. An avalanche of rocks fell to the ground.

When Ash and Kellyn arrived at the mouth of

the chamber, they found it completely sealed. If they couldn't break through those rocks, the client would escape with Riolu!

Kellyn thought fast. "Capture on. Vatonage!" he shouted, aiming at a wild Donphan. "Capture complete! Donphan, use Rollout!" The armored Donphan had thick tusks. It barreled through the wall of rocks. Ash and Kellyn raced into the chamber. But the client was gone — and all ten tunnels were sealed up by rocks.

"They're tons of boulders blocking every passageway!" Kellyn complained. "And Riolu can only be behind one of them."

By the time they unblocked all the tunnels, the client and Riolu would be long gone. They had to guess right the first time. Which means they couldn't take a chance on *guessing*.

"Okay, Riolu, tell me," Ash said, closing his eyes and trying to sense the Pokémon. "Where are you?"

The answer flashed through his mind. "This one!" Ash said triumphantly, pointing at the closest of the pathways. "Riolu's in there."

"Now, Donphan. Rollout," Kellyn commanded.

Donphan smashed through the rocks. Within moments, they were on the other side, face to face with the client.

"All right, *stop!*" Ash ordered him.

"It's all over," Kellyn added.

The client turned to face them. He had nowhere else to run. "But how could you have figured out which way we went?!"

"Simple. Riolu told me," Ash said proudly.

The client didn't understand. "Told you?" He couldn't imagine that Riolu was communicating with Ash. To him, the Pokémon was just property. Something to poke and prod and *use*.

"Riolu's coming with *us* now," Kellyn said.

"Not a chance," the client shot back. "Quick, Aggron, Double-Edge!"

"Donphan, Horn Attack!" Kellyn countered.

The two Pokémon ran toward each other. Donphan's Horn Attack was stronger. The massive Aggron stumbled backward, crashing into the client. He lurched off-balance and dropped the glass case.

"Riolu!" Ash cried. He snatched the case off the ground. There was a dial on the front. He twisted it, and the field immobilizing Riolu disappeared. The Pokémon came back to life. Ash was overjoyed. "You're okay! Riolu, you're okay!"

Riolu threw its arms around Ash.

"Riolu belongs to *me*!" the client raged. "Aggron, Hyper Beam!"

A ball of fire shot out of the Aggron. But Riolu was ready. He fired an Aura Sphere. A blue ball of energy screamed toward the Aggron. It met the Hyper Beam in midair. They collided with loud crack and a blast of foul black smoke.

"Pikachu, Volt Tackle!" Ash ordered.

Pikachu generated a wide energy field. It electrified the Aggron, who tipped over and collapsed. Right on top of the client.

"I'd say you're done," Kellyn told him. "Give up!"

The client balled his fists and smacked them into the ground. He snarled at Ash and Kellyn. He yelled at his Aggron, but there was nothing he could do. The Aggron was unconscious, and the client was trapped beneath it.

Which meant they could leave him behind.

And Riolu would finally be free.

Chapter 11

Hunter J's client may have gotten caught, but Hunter J was still out there causing trouble. Her ship coasted high over the desert.

"Here, Commander J," her lead henchman said, "our next mission."

Hunter J gave him a greedy smile. She was ready to put the Riolu disaster behind her. There were plenty of other powerful Pokémon out there, just waiting to be caught. "Set a course for heading two seven five!"

Hunter J didn't know it, but her ship was charging straight toward Team Rocket's hot air balloon. Team Rocket may have lost their chance to catch Riolu, but they were determined not to let Hunter J get away.

"Team Rocket to block!" Jessie cheered, as the balloon sailed closer and closer to the ship.

"When it comes to winning the high stakes game, it's all in the moves."

"We've got them, as this proves," James boasted.

"On the wind!" Jessie cheered.

"Past the stars!" James added.

Meowth peeked his head over the side of the balloon basket. "What a groove!"

Jessie watched Hunter J's ship impatiently. She was certain this time her plan would work. "Bringing chaos at a breakneck pace," she chanted.

"Dashing hope, putting fear in its place!" James cried.

"A loser by any other name's just as lost!" Jessie crowed.

"You're gonna be sorry that our paths have crossed!" James shouted.

Jessie pumped her fist in the air. "Jessie!"

James laughed at the fools on Hunter J's ship. "James!"

"Meowth's da name!" Meowth jeered. His eyes went wide as Hunter J's ship suddenly disappeared. "Hey, we're not troo yet! Where'd ya *go?*"

But the ship hadn't *gone* anywhere. Hunter J had turned on the cloaking device, making the ship invisible. So Team Rocket didn't see it coming. They just *felt* it, when it crashed right into them. Their balloon exploded with a deafening *POP*. They panicked, waving their arms and legs as if they could fly.

But they couldn't.

Team Rocket plummeted toward the earth. "We're blasting off agaaaaaaaaain!"

Far, far below, on a cliff overlooking Riolu's kingdom, things were much more peaceful. As the sun dipped beneath the horizon, Ash and his friends returned Riolu to his rightful home. The kindly old man who had raised Riolu embraced the Pokémon gratefully. He had been afraid he would never see Riolu again.

"So thanks to all of you, mission safely accomplished," Kellyn told Ash and his friends. "You were great!"

Solana grinned at Ash. "Don't forget, I *told* you Ash would be a big help."

Ash blushed. "Ah, it wasn't much."

But Riolu's Trainer knew he had Ash to thank for getting the Pokémon back. "And on behalf of the many wonderful people who live in our kingdom, I wish to convey my sincere gratitude for returning our Riolu to us," he said.

"Thanks!" Brock said. "And since Riolu's first group of captors have been arrested as well, you can return home without worry."

Dawn was sorry to say good-bye to the little Pokémon. "Riolu, you take care!" she told him.

Ash handed Riolu its wooden doll. Riolu and its trainer looked surprised that Ash had rescued it, too. But Ash knew how important the doll was to Riolu. "And you take good care of this, too," he said.

He shivered, as Riolu's Aura zapped him, probably for the last time.

Dawn noticed the strange look on Ash's face. "Riolu's Aura, right?" she guessed.

Ash smiled sadly. "Yeah, that was just Riolu telling me thanks. That's what you said, right?" he asked the Pokémon.

"Riolu!" the Pokémon chirped.

Ash knew that Riolu's kingdom needed the Pokémon to protect it. So this had to be good-bye. But he was still sorry to leave his new friend behind. "I'm never gonna forget you, Riolu," Ash promised. "Not *ever.*"

And he never would.